P9-DUM-410

MONICA BROWN

WITHDRAWN

LOLA LEVINE

Drama Queen

ILLUSTRATED BY
Angela Dominguez

LITTLE, BROWN AND COMPANY
New York • Boston

This book is a work of fiction. Names, characters, places, and incidents are the product of the author's imagination or are used fictitiously. Any resemblance to actual events, locales, or persons, living or dead, is coincidental.

Text copyright © 2016 by Monica Brown
Interior Artwork copyright © 2016 by Angela Dominguez
Crown—Thibault Geffroy Paris, FR 2011

All rights reserved. In accordance with the U.S. Copyright Act of 1976, the scanning, uploading, and electronic sharing of any part of this book without the permission of the publisher is unlawful piracy and theft of the author's intellectual property. If you would like to use material from the book (other than for review purposes), prior written permission must be obtained by contacting the publisher at permissions@hbgusa.com. Thank you for your support of the author's rights.

Little, Brown and Company

Hachette Book Group
1290 Avenue of the Americas, New York, NY 10104
Visit us at lb-kids.com

Little, Brown and Company is a division of Hachette Book Group, Inc.
The Little, Brown name and logo are trademarks of Hachette Book Group, Inc.

The publisher is not responsible for websites (or their content) that are not owned by the publisher.

First Edition: January 2016

Library of Congress Cataloging-in-Publication Data

Brown, Monica, 1969–
Lola Levine, drama queen / Monica Brown.
pages cm
Summary: "Lola Levine is given a non-speaking part after getting stage fright during her class play audition. She saves the play after a couple of obstacles with the help of her grandmother"— Provided by publisher.
ISBN 978-0-316-25843-2 (hardback) — ISBN 978-0-316-25839-5 (ebook) [1. Stage fright—Fiction. 2. Theater—Fiction. 3. Schools—Fiction. 4. Family life—Fiction.] I. Title.
PZ7.B816644Loj 2015
[Fic]—dc23
2014042735

10 9 8 7 6 5 4 3 2

RRD-C

Printed in the United States of America

For Nikki S.
Mary D.
Donn H.

with gratitude

CONTENTS

Chapter Six

Chapter Seven

Chapter Eight

Dear *Diario*,

I can't sleep. I want to juggle my soccer ball, but I'm pretty sure that would wake everyone else up. I could paint on the walls of my room, but I'm not feeling full of what my artist dad calls "creative expression." What I am feeling full of is energy—inside and out.

Sometimes my thoughts are like monkeys jumping up and down in my head saying, "Ooh-ooh, aah-aah!" Sometimes my monkeys are swinging from trees.

I'm excited for school tomorrow because Ms. Garcia says there will be a surprise. I *love* surprises. I can't imagine anything better than the last surprise, which involved worms and garbage.

My monkeys are getting tired.

Shalom and *buenas noches*,
Lola Levine

Chapter One
Walk, Don't Run

My name is Lola Levine, and the truth is little brothers are sometimes a pain. At least mine is.

"Lola! Zola! Granola! It's time to get up!" yells Ben right in my ear.

"Ouch," I say, and pull the covers over my head. Usually I am up way before Ben. Why am I so tired? Oh yeah—I couldn't sleep.

"Cow barn," I mumble into my pillow. I can't say "darn" because that's a word Mom would rather I didn't use.

"It just doesn't sound nice," she says.

"Dolores! Boris! Morris! Wake up!" Ben keeps going with his awful rhymes until I'm up and out of bed.

"Ben," I say, "don't try to rhyme, you moldy lime." I like words a lot, and I'm good at rhyming them. I'm much better at rhyming than my brother, Ben, in my opinion, and I have *lots* of opinions.

"Dolores!" Ben shouts again. He knows I don't like being called that—I like my nickname Lola much better. My middle name is Esther and I like that. According to Grandma Levine, my *bubbe*, Esther means "star" in Hebrew.

"Wanna hear a joke, Lola?" Ben asks. He likes telling jokes. "What do kitties eat for dessert?"

"I don't know," I grumble.

"*Mice* cream!" he says. "Get it? Get it? 'Mice' instead of 'ice.'"

"I get it," I say. Ever since Mom and Dad agreed that we could get a kitty this summer, Ben's started with the cat jokes.

I stretch my hands toward the ceiling. If I jump up, I can almost touch the stars Dad and I painted on the ceiling a few weeks ago. It was really fun—until I got paint in my eyes. After that, Mom made

sure both Dad and I wore goggles when we decided to paint ceilings. Ben thought our paint goggles looked cool, so now he wears them even when he isn't painting. They're big and round, and I think they make him look like a bug.

Now Ben's trying to touch his hands to the ceiling, too, only he thinks it will be easier if he jumps off my dresser.

Thwunk! He lands on the floor, hard. *Thwunk! Kerplunk!* He tries again.

This time Dad yells. "What's going on up there? Hurry or you'll be late for school!" He and Mom take turns driving us to school each morning.

Mom must have an early assignment for the newspaper, because she's gone by the time we get downstairs. Dad's making pancakes, but it's taking really long because he is trying to make them into different shapes. Dad's an artist who believes in creative expression—even with pancakes. Sometimes, when I am upset, he gives me a piece of paper and a pencil and tells me to draw my feelings. I like art, but I like words better than pictures when it comes to feelings. Finally, the pancakes are ready.

"Mine looks like an ear," Ben complains.

"It's a whale," Dad says. "See the blueberry eye?"

"I thought that was an earring," Ben says.

I'm not sure what my pancake is, but I don't want to hurt Dad's feelings, so I say,

"Looks great, Dad," and bite into what I think is a snail. I think Dad's better with paint.

In the driveway, we get into Dad's orange car—what Dad calls his people mover. I guess the people mover doesn't move very fast, because it takes forever to warm up and we are late for school. I get sent to the office for a late slip.

"Hi, Principal Blot!" I say, peeking into her office. Principal Blot isn't just my principal. She's also the mother of my super best friend, Josh Blot. She looks up from her desk.

"Good morning, Lola," she says with a frown. Principal Blot frowns a lot, especially around me.

"Are you in trouble?" she asks.

"No!" I say. "I'm just late. It's because my dad was making creative pancakes, and our people mover was slow." Principal Blot looks up at the ceiling and takes a deep breath. Her ceiling is plain white.

"I've got stars on my ceiling, Principal Blot. You should come over and see them—"

"Lola!" Principal Blot interrupts. "Aren't you late for class?"

"Yes," I say.

"So, shouldn't you get going?" she asks.

"Yes!" I say, and start to sprint to class. But I have my backpack on, and I guess I forgot to zip it, because everything spills out.

"Lola! No running in the halls," Principal Blot says. "You know better than that."

"Sorry, Principal Blot. I forgot. I hope you're not exasperated, Principal Blot." My mom uses the word "exasperated" a lot. She says it is a nice way of saying that you're annoyed. It's a cool word, in my opinion.

"Lola," Principal Blot says. "If you don't get going right now, I promise I *will* be exasperated. Now walk, *don't run*, to class."

Chapter Two
Wave like Wheat

Before I go to lunch, I leave a note on Ms. Garcia's chair.

Dear Ms. Garcia,

Are we going to find out about the surprise today? I'm soooooo tired of waiting. You told me not to ask again in class, but I'm not in class right now, I'm outside playing soccer (I hope—I don't actually know because I'm not actually outside yet), and I think you are eating lunch at your desk, reading my note. Unless you have yard duty. If you do, please close this note right now, because I might be *in* class when you find this note and you might be exasperated.

Shalom,
Lola Levine

When I come back from lunch, Ms. Garcia is smiling and I don't see my note, so I guess she isn't exasperated with me. Ms. Garcia is the best.

"Are you ready for the surprise?" Ms. Garcia asks.

"Yes!" we say. Finally. I couldn't even concentrate during the soccer game over lunch. Alyssa Goldstein scored on me, which I disliked very much.

"For the next eight weeks, we are going to have a special drama class, with a special drama teacher who will come twice a week," Ms. Garcia says. "At the end of the class, we will have a class play!"

A new teacher? I'm not sure how I feel about that. Ms. Garcia is my favorite teacher ever. And I'm not sure what a drama class involves.

I *have* heard Mom use the word

"dramatic." Last time my grandma Levine visited, for example, I heard Mom ask Dad, "Why is your mother so dramatic?" I didn't know what she meant, so I borrowed Mom's dictionary. There were a lot of different definitions for "dramatic," but I picked the ones that said:

1. extreme and sudden
2. attracting attention; causing people to look and listen

Mom must have been talking about the way Bubbe hugs *extremely* tight. And now that I think about it, Bubbe does get a lot of attention, mostly because of how she dresses. She looks like a rainbow and always wears colorful shawls and scarves. I think she is why my dad became an artist.

And it *is* easy to listen carefully when Bubbe talks, because she talks really, really loud. I talk loud, too. Especially on the soccer field. And sometimes in class. Last year, when I was in first grade, I used to get in trouble a lot for being loud. My teacher would say, "Lola Levine, use your *inside* voice."

"This IS my INSIDE voice," I always answered. For some reason, my teacher didn't like that answer very much. But it seemed like when *she* talked to *me*, she always used a voice you could hear all the way outside—it was very confusing.

Ms. Garcia lines us up, and we get ready to go to the gym.

"Psst. Josh!" I say. "Do you think I'm dramatic?"

"Definitely," Josh whispers back, smiling. We get to the gym, where our new teacher is waiting.

"Students," Ms. Garcia says, "give a warm Northland Elementary welcome to Ms. Tinkle." When I see Ms. Tinkle, I'm not sure where to look. I've never seen someone with so many sparkles. She has on big, shiny butterfly earrings and about a hundred bracelets, which click and clang together when she moves her arms. And guess what? Ms. Tinkle moves her arms a lot.

"Good afternoon, students!" she says with a wave of her arms. She sort of reminds me of a butterfly, actually, because

she is wearing a big orange shirt and green pants. I see that she's wearing sandals, too, with purple glitter toenail polish. She even has rings on her toes! Wait until I tell Mom.

"Good afternoon, Ms. Tinkle," we all say. I think I say it a little louder than everyone else, because she looks straight at me.

"Welcome to drama class, everyone! We'll be working together this spring. The word 'drama' comes from the Greek word for action, and here you will learn to act and tell a story onstage." It's hard to pay attention because I'm thinking about Ms. Tinkle—about her name, actually. Tinkle. It reminds me of something, but I'm not sure what. Then I remember a silly rhyme my mom made up and used to sing to me:

"My little Lola, with her smiling dimples,
Tell Mommy when it's time to tinkle!
My little Lola, bumblebee,
Tell Mommy when it's time to wee!"

All of a sudden, I really, *really* have to go to the bathroom.

"Ms. Tinkle! Ms. Tinkle!" I raise my hand. "May I be excused? I have to tinkle— I mean pee." Did I just say "tinkle"? Cow barn, I think. I should have said "use the bathroom."

Makayla Miller laughs and whispers something to Alyssa. When they whisper, it's usually about me, and I dislike that very much. I see other kids giggling, too, and even Josh thinks it's funny. Ms. Tinkle does not look too happy.

"Fine," she says. "You may use the restroom."

Then Juan Gomez raises his hand and says, "Ms. Tinkle, I need to tinkle, too. May I be excused?" Now everyone is laughing.

"Silence!" Ms. Tinkle says. "I'll have you know that the word 'tinkle' is a sound, not only an action." To prove her point, she waves her arms, and the little bells on one of her bracelets make a tinkling sound.

When Juan and I get back from the bathroom, the class is in a big circle, and Ms. Tinkle's cheeks are red. I feel bad because I think I'm the reason everyone laughed at her name, and I sure know how that feels: not very good.

"Okay, class, let's warm up," says Ms. Tinkle.

"I can lead warm-ups!" I say. "I'm the captain of my soccer team, the Orange Smoothies, and I lead warm-ups all the time!"

"Nobody cares, Lola," says Alyssa. I try to follow Dad's advice to ignore people when they are being mean.

"We are going to warm up with improv games today, class," Ms. Tinkle says.

"Why do we have to warm up for drama?" Juan asks.

"Well," Ms. Tinkle says, "we need to warm up our acting muscles!"

I don't understand. I don't know what "improv" means, and I have no clue which of my muscles is my acting one.

"I'm not talking about the muscles in your body. I'm talking about warming up your mind and letting your imagination run free!" Ms. Tinkle explains. "Improvisation teaches you how to create without any preparation. You have to think on your feet. Now raise your hands in the air! Wave like wheat."

"Wave like wheat?" I whisper to Josh. "How does wheat wave?"

"Like this," he says, and waves his hands and bops me on the head.

"Now buzz like bees!" Ms. Tinkle says, and the whole class buzzes, which is fun until people start poking one another and yelling, "You've been stung!"

Alyssa doesn't like that game, I guess, because she yells, "Lola just poked me in the eye, and my mom isn't going to like this!" I actually poked Alyssa's *cheek*, which is very different, in my opinion. Ms. Tinkle quickly tells us to pretend we are frogs, ribbiting and hopping around, but things get a little crazy when Juan tries to leap over Josh and ends up knocking over a trash can. A *full* trash can, which includes the grape juice someone didn't finish at lunch and a smelly tuna sandwich.

Ms. Tinkle, who is looking a little less twinkly, says, "Statues! Stand perfectly still and SILENT like statues." Then, with a tinkle and a clink and a clang of her bracelets, she walks toward the door of the gym, where Ms. Garcia is waiting.

"I think we've had enough drama, I mean, learned enough *about* drama today," Ms. Tinkle says. "Class dismissed."

Chapter Three

Sizzle, Pop

On Friday, we have drama class again, and Ms. Tinkle has us do even more exercises. She explains that we will be "mirroring" another person. Unfortunately, Alyssa is my other person, and she's got a great big frown on her face.

"Remember," Ms. Tinkle says, "one of you is the mirror and one of you is the person, and the mirror has to reflect what the person is doing."

"You're the mirror, Lola," Alyssa says. "I'm the person." Then she flips her hair, so I do, too, but I don't have nearly as much hair to flip.

"Are you making fun of me?" she grumbles.

"No, I'm mirroring you," I say.

She raises her arm, so I raise my arm. She moves her feet, and I try to move my feet in the same way, but I'm bored, so I do a little jump and spin.

"Lola Levine, you are so weird!" Alyssa says with her hands on her hips.

"I'm not weird. I'm *dramatic*," I say with my hands on my hips just like hers. I think of the definition in Mom's dictionary. "I attract attention!"

"Yeah, because you're weird. And loud, too. *I'm* going to be an actress when I grow up," she says, stomping her foot. I stomp my foot, too.

"Well, maybe I'll be an actress, too," I say, raising my voice. "My middle name means 'star,' you know."

Just then, Ms. Tinkle raises her arms and says, "STOP! It's time for our next activity. Everyone lie down on the floor."

I'm happy the mirror game is done, and I go lie down next to Josh.

"Now, students, this is called the popcorn game. I want everyone to pretend they're popcorn kernels and the floor is a great big pan filled with oil."

"Yuck," I whisper to Josh.

"Lola! Pay attention!" Ms. Tinkle says. I guess I have a loud whisper.

"Now, students," Ms. Tinkle says, "imagine the pan is getting sizzling hot."

"Aaaaaaaaaaaaaaaah! I'm burning up," I scream, because I want Ms. Tinkle to know I'm good at acting.

"Please, no screaming, Lola. You'll scare the kindergartners next door," Ms. Tinkle says. Ben is in kindergarten, and it would take more than a few screams to scare him, I think.

"Improvise!" Ms. Tinkle says. "You are *popcorn kernels*—what do you do?" Alyssa jumps up and claps her hands.

"That's right, Alyssa!" Ms. Tinkle says. "You pop! Well done." Soon everyone starts to jump and pop and clap, and

it does sound pretty cool. I wish I had thought of popping.

I'm happy when the bell rings and drama class is over.

I go to Josh's house after school.

Josh and I have lots of fun playing soccer in his backyard, but we have to be extra careful not to smush the plants in Josh's mom's vegetable garden.

"Lola," Josh says, "can you wave like wheat while dribbling a soccer ball?"

"No!" I say. "But I can buzz like a bee! *Bzzzzzzzzzz!*" We try to get Josh's cat, Milo, to play soccer with us, but he'd rather nap in the sun.

"Guess what, Lola?" Josh asks between soccer juggles.

"What?" I say.

"I'm really excited about the class play," he says.

"It will be fun," I say. I'm secretly hoping to be the star!

After a while, we get hot and hungry and go inside for a snack.

"Would you like something salty or something sweet?" Principal Blot asks us.

"Salty," Josh says.

"Sweet," I say.

Josh gets celery sticks sprinkled with salt, and I get carrots. I have to admit they are pretty good carrots, so I tell Principal Blot that very thing.

"These are the sweetest carrots I've

ever tasted, Principal Blot—I mean Josh's mom!" I say.

"You think so?" she replies.

"Yes! Can I have some more?" I ask, and then remember to add, "Please?"

"Of course. I grow them in my own garden!" she says, and then Principal Blot does something I've never ever seen her do. She smiles.

Chapter Four
Bubble-Gum Ice Cream

Dear *Diario*,

It's been a loooooooooong month. We
have drama class twice a week, and I
still can't decide if I like it. Yesterday,

Ms. Tinkle told us that we are going to have to *audition* for the class play. "Audition" means "try out." I've been to soccer tryouts, so hopefully this won't be too hard.

The play is called *Forest Gifts* and is about the creatures that live in the woods—animals and fairies. I never liked fairies much—what do they do besides be tiny and fly around, anyway?

Shalom,
Lola Levine

"Guess what, Lola?" my brother says on Saturday morning. "Mira is coming over today!" Mira is really sweet, even if her older sister *is* Alyssa Goldstein.

"What are you guys going to do?" I ask Ben.

"Mom's taking us to the park and Ice Cream Palace!" Ben says. Ice Cream Palace has about three zillion flavors of ice cream—it's the best ice cream in town, in my opinion.

"Lucky!" I tell Ben, but I'm not too jealous, because I'm going to spend the morning painting with Dad.

"Ready to create?" Dad asks.

"Yes!" I say, and we walk out to his studio in the backyard.

When I come out of Dad's studio a long time later, I see Ben and Mira in the

backyard. I notice that Ben's and Mira's lips are...*blue*.

"Blee blot blubble blum blice bleam!" Ben says, his mouth full of chewing gum.

"You got bubble-gum ice cream?" I say.

"Blee blar blaving bla blubble blowing blontest!" says Mira.

"Have fun," I say, "and let the biggest bubble win!"

I know I need to work on my audition, but first I need Mom's advice.

"Mom," I say. "I need help."

"With what?" Mom asks.

"My audition for Ms. Tinkle. We have two minutes to audition with a song, dance, or monologue. Ms. Tinkle said a monologue is the expression of a character's mental thoughts."

"Aren't all thoughts mental?" Mom laughs.

"I said the very same thing, but she told me not to interrupt. She said we can choose our own characters or she'll give us a monologue to read. What should I do?"

"What do *you* want to do?" asks Mom.

"Mom," I say. "Why do you always answer my questions with another question?"

"Because I think you're pretty smart," Mom says with a smile, "and I like to hear your answers."

"Well, I don't really know how to dance, and I'm not used to singing, but I have a lot of mental thoughts," I say.

"Yes," Mom says, "but you're supposed to be a character, not yourself, right?"

"Right," I say. "So what character should I be?"

"How about another famous Dolores, like Dolores Huerta?"

"That's a great idea!" I tell Mom. Dolores Huerta was a leader who helped farmworkers in California—I learned about her from Ms. Garcia. "Didn't Dolores Huerta always say *¡Sí, se puede!*—'Yes, we can!'—to workers trying to make their jobs better?"

"Yes, she did," Mom says.

"I'm going to be Dolores Huerta! I'm going to start working on my monologue right now—thanks, Mom!" I say, and give her a hug. I start up the stairs, where Ben nearly knocks me over.

"Lola! I need your help," he says, taking my hand and leading me to his room.

"Where's Mira?" I ask.

"Shhhhhhhhhhh!" he says.

"Why are you shushing me?"

"Because I'm in trouble," says Ben.

"What did you do?" I say. I see Mira sitting on the floor of Ben's room, playing with his Legos. Oh no.

"Hi, Lola!" Mira says with a smile. I guess she doesn't realize that she's missing a great big chunk of hair on the side of her head. "I won the bubble-gum blowing contest, Lola! But I got my bubble gum stuck in my hair, so Ben cut it out."

"Wow," I say, but I'm looking at the space where a chunk of hair is…missing.

"Can you fix it?" whispers Ben.

"Hmmmmm," I say. "I guess I can try." But I'm a little worried. The last time I tried to cut hair, it was my own, and Mom wasn't too happy about it. I liked the way my spiky hair looked, but I sure didn't like being teased about it. I go get a brush and some rubber bands and ribbons and try to find a hairstyle that covers Mira's bald patch. It's not working, but Mira likes the ponytails I've put all over her head.

"Maybe we can paint it," I say.

"Yes!" says Josh.

"I like purple!" says Mira, but as soon as I'm done mixing up the color, we hear Mom's voice.

"Ben! Mira! Come downstairs. Mrs. Goldstein is here to pick up Mira."

I feel like hiding under my bed, but instead I walk downstairs with Mira and Ben. I've never met Mrs. Goldstein, but I'm not surprised when I do.

"Mira!" she says. "What happened to your beautiful hair?!" She puts her hands on her hips and looks just like Alyssa when she's mad. Mira must be more like Mr. Goldstein.

"It's still beautiful," I say, trying to help. "There's just less of it."

Ben explains what happened and says he's super sorry. Mom apologizes, too, and offers to take Mira to the hairdresser, but Mrs. Goldstein says, "No, thank you. It's time to go, Mira."

"But I want to stay," says Mira.

"You can come back again soon," says Mom, smiling at Mira.

"We'll see," says Mrs. Goldstein, and she and Mira are out the door.

"What is it with you two and scissors?" Mom asks with a sigh.

Ben is upset for the rest of the weekend. I know this because Sunday is sunny and nice, and Ben is sitting inside on the couch wearing his paint goggles *and* his soccer mouth guard. I decide to cheer him up with a cat joke.

"Ben, why was the kitty so grumpy?" I ask.

Ben shrugs.

"Because he was in a bad mewd," I say, trying to get Ben to laugh.

He just takes out his mouth guard and says, "I'm in a bad mewd, too."

On Monday morning, Ben and I run into Alyssa and Mira on the way into school. Mira's hair is pretty much gone. She has a super-short cut, but at least now everything is the same length as the part Ben cut off.

"Mira!" Ben says. "You look cool!" Then he asks, "Can I touch your head?"

"Sure," Mira says, but Alyssa grabs her sister's hand and pulls.

"Come on, Mira, we're leaving."

"It was an accident!" I yell to Alyssa, just in time for Principal Blot to hear me as she walks out of her office.

"Lola," she says, "must you always be so loud?" That's me, I think, Lola the Loud.

Chapter Five
Auditions

The rest of the week I spend lots of time writing and practicing my Dolores Huerta monologue. At night, I practice in front of my parents.

"My name is Dolores Huerta, and I work
for what is right.
I use my words to organize and fight.
I believe in the people who work in the
fields
And bring food to our table each night.
They should be safe and make enough
to live—
We should thank them for all they
give.
When people think we can't win, I just
say, 'iSí, se puede!'—'Yes, we can!'
And send my message to every child,
woman, and man."

"It's awesome!" says Dad as I take
a bow.

"Wow!" says Mom. "I just love your rhymes, my sweet Lola. You have a way with words."

"Just like her mom," says Dad, giving Mom a kiss on the cheek. I sure hope he's right.

Dear *Diario*,

Tomorrow is the audition for *Forest Gifts*, and I'm really excited about it! I just know it's going to go great. The monkeys in my mind aren't swinging from trees, they are up onstage, taking a bow!

Shalom,
Lola Levine

On the day of the audition, I wear my lucky shirt, which says I'M THE REASON YOUR COACH MAKES YOU PRACTICE SO MUCH. It has my soccer number on the back—1. I watch as the other students stand at the front of the gym and take their turn. Makayla is dressed head to toe in pink, and she dances and sings and twirls and swirls until I'm dizzy just looking at her.

Alyssa wears fairy wings while she gives her monologue. She says she's Ariel, but not the mermaid. She's Ariel, a fairy from Shakespeare. Ms. Tinkle claps very loudly after Alyssa's audition and tells us we should all know who Shakespeare is.

"He's the greatest dramatist of all time," she says with a tinkle of her bracelets.

"I thought he wrote plays," I say.

"That's the same thing, Lola!" Makayla says with a smirk.

Next it's Josh's turn. He doesn't have anything prepared, so Ms. Tinkle hands him a monologue. I cross my fingers that he does okay. He doesn't look too nervous, though.

"Go, Josh!" I say, but Ms. Tinkle shushes me. Then he starts to read:

"I am the King of the Forest, mighty and brave.
With my queen I protect and save.
Join us for this magical forest tale,
And through fairy dreams we will sail.
Learn about all of nature's gifts
As four seasons pass and shift."

Josh's voice starts out a little quiet, but then he gets louder and better, and when he finishes, at first no one says anything. Then he takes a big, *dramatic* bow, and everyone claps. Loudly.

"You did great, Josh!" I say when he walks back to the group.

"Thanks, Lola," Josh says, giving me a high five.

We watch the other tryouts, and then Ms. Tinkle calls my name. As I walk up to the stage, I start feeling kind of weird and hot. My heart feels like it's trying to thump out of my chest, and when I turn to face everyone, I freeze.

"Go ahead, Lola," Ms. Tinkle says.

"My name is…," I say, but all of a sudden I can't remember who I'm supposed to be! I feel a drip down my back—I'm sweating like I've just played a whole game of soccer.

"My name is...," I say again, and I just can't think.

Ms. Tinkle smiles at me and says, "It's okay, Lola, we all forget our lines sometimes. Would you like more time?"

All I really want to do is get down off the stage, so I say, "No, thank you." And I walk back down to where the rest of the class is standing. I think that even Alyssa and Makayla feel sorry for me, because they don't whisper one word.

"Olivia Lopez!" Ms. Tinkle says, and luckily, the class turns to look at her.

"Forget about it, Lola," Josh says when

the bell rings for recess. "Let's go play soccer."

"Okay," I say, but I can't even pretend to smile. At least I don't cry until I get home, when Mom's arms are wrapped around me tight.

The next day, Ms. Tinkle posts the cast list on the bulletin board outside the gym just before lunch.

"Remember," she says as we all crowd around the list, "a great drama teacher once said, 'There are no small parts, only small actors.'"

I stop reading right there. Squirrel #2? What kind of role is that? I run outside

CAST

King of the Forest—Josh Blot

Queen of the Forest—Alyssa Goldstein

Fairy Princess—Makayla Miller

Bluebird #1—Olivia Lopez

Bluebird #2—Emily Kang

Squirrel #1—Juan Gomez

Squirrel #2—Lola Levine

and keep running around the playground until I hear the bell. I think about my audition and how I froze and forgot my lines, and I feel even worse. Mom called it stage fright and said that everyone has it once in a while, but I'm no scaredy-cat!

There's only one thing that will make me feel better, so I find Josh after school.

"Want to go to the park and play soccer?"

"I can't today, Lola," he says, looking away.

"Why not?" I ask.

"Because he's rehearsing the King and Queen of the Forest scenes with *me*," Alyssa says with her usual smirk.

"Okay," I say, hoping I won't cry before

I see Mom in the car line. Instead of crying, though, I decide to write to Grandma Levine. As soon as I get home, I write my letter.

Dear Bubbe:

How are you doing over there in Florida? Is it sunny and nice? Have you seen any turtles on the beach?

    I am okay. Well, actually, I'm not okay at all. I'm in a play, but I don't have any words to act. I am a squirrel, and not even Squirrel #1. I am Squirrel #2, which means all I get to do is carry the nuts to the King and Queen of the Forest. At least I don't have any lines to forget.

All I have to say about that is *double cow barn*, you know, because I'm not supposed to say double darn. I miss you.

Love and shalom and
a great big hug,
Lola Levine, Squirrel (#2)

Chapter Six
The Big Surprise

The days pass slowly. We have play rehearsal three days a week now, and I get to watch Josh and Alyssa on the thrones that I helped decorate. I feel really grumpy and jealous, but I do have fun painting sets, and I like my fluffy, furry squirrel costume. It's brown and soft and matches the color of my hair.

Finally, the weekend of the play comes. Our performance will be Saturday night, and on Friday, Mom, Dad, Ben, and I have dinner together. After dinner, Mom makes us *batidos de plátano*, banana shakes. My mom's banana shakes are so yummy. She just puts milk, bananas, ice, and cinnamon in the blender, and we have a special dessert! While we slurp, I ask Ben how Mira is doing.

"Bad," Ben says. "People keep telling her she looks like a boy because her hair is so short."

"What's wrong with that?" I say, running my hands through my own shortish hair and looking at Ben's and Dad's pony-tails. "Boys and girls should look however they want!"

"I agree," says Dad.

"Me too," says Mom, even though her hair goes all the way down to her waist.

Riiiiiiiiing! Riiiiiiiiiiiiing!

"I wonder who it is," Mom says, sipping her shake.

Riiiiiiiiiiiing! Riiiiiiiiiing!

"It could be important," Dad says, and picks up the phone. "Oh, hi! Mom, how are you?...You want to talk to Lola? She's right here."

"Bubbe!" I say. She must have gotten my letter. "Yeah! I was wondering when you would call."

"How's my little squirrel?" she asks.

"Much better now!" I say.

Just then, the doorbell rings.

"I think you should answer the door,"
Bubbe says.

"Wow, Bubbe," I say, "you have good

ears if you can hear the doorbell over the phone!" I walk over to answer the door while I tell Grandma how happy I am that she called. I open the door, and guess what?

My very own grandma Levine, my *bubbe*, is standing right there, talking on her purple cell phone. To me.

"Yeah! Yeah! Yeah!" I yell. Everyone comes running, and Mom, Dad, Ben, and I all hug Grandma Levine at once.

"What a wonderful surprise, Mom," Dad says.

"Perfect timing, Ruth!" Mom says. "Now you can come to Lola's play tomorrow night."

"Lola," Grandma says, "I booked my flight as soon as I got your letter."

"But I'm not even the star," I tell Grandma.

"But you're MY star, Lola Esther Levine," Grandma says.

"Grandma! Grandma!" Ben says, jumping up and down. "Want to hear a cat joke?"

"Of course, Benny Boy!" says Bubbe.

"What did the kitty eat for breakfast?" Ben asks.

"What?" says Grandma Levine.

"Mice Krispies!" says Ben, and he jumps up and down some more.

I'm so happy Bubbe is here. Ben is, too.

"I've got lots to tell you, Grandma," says Ben. "Especially about my friend Mira and the bubble-gum disaster."

"And I've got lots more to tell you, too," I say.

"Good, because I've got big ears for listening and big arms for hugging!" says Bubbe, wrapping us up in her arms. "Let's make some apple tea and have a good talk."

"Yum!" I say, because Bubbe's apple tea is full of honey and spices and lots of good stuff. We make it together, and the whole house smells delicious.

Chapter Seven
Showtime!

On the morning of the play, I crawl into bed with Grandma Levine.

"Bubbe," I say. "I'm worried."

"Why, Lola Esther?" she asks with a smile.

"Because you flew here all the way from Florida to see me in the play, and I don't even have any lines. I'm not important."

"But, Lola, everyone is important, most ESPECIALLY you."

"Well, Ms. Tinkle doesn't think so— she thinks I'm afraid to be onstage, and I'm not! And these two girls, Alyssa and Makayla, are the stars of the show, and the truth is I dislike them very much. They aren't ever nice to me."

"Are you nice to them?" Bubbe asks me. I think about it.

"I try to be," I say.

"Well, that's what's most important, my sweet. You are smart and special, and I'm sure Ms. Tinkle knows that. We can't

always get what we want at the exact time
we want it."

"Do you think I'm dramatic, Bubbe?
Or am I just loud?"

"Lola Esther," Bubbe says with a smile
and a wink, "the truth is you are both—just
like me."

Later, when Dad and Bubbe drop me off
at school, Bubbe blows me a kiss out the
window. She's dressed up for the play,
with a long purple dress and a peacock
shawl with gold fringe. She wears gold
shoes to match, of course.

When I walk into the gym, Ms. Tinkle
stops me first thing.

"Lola! We have a crisis. Juan is sick, so you have to say his lines," she says. "Here they are—learn them!"

"You mean I'm Squirrel Number One now?" I ask.

"Yes!" Ms. Tinkle says. "You are Squirrel Number One AND Number Two! Just remember, Lola, the show must go on!" And then she's off to adjust Makayla's fairy wings.

Suddenly, I feel sick. I can barely breathe in my fur. I sink into the corner, holding the paper with my new lines, and Josh walks over to me.

"Josh!" Alyssa yells. "Come back. I need you to rehearse with me." He ignores her.

"You're going to do great," Josh says, looking very *kingly* with his crown.

"Thanks, Josh," I say, "but I only have an hour to memorize my lines, and what if I freeze again?"

"You can do it, Lola," Josh says. "You are the smartest person I know, and since when is Lola Levine afraid of anything?"

"Josh Blot," I say, "you are a super best friend."

I am going to show Ms. Tinkle and everyone else that I, Lola Levine, can act and be dramatic, even up on a big stage.

I go over my lines again and again until Ms. Tinkle says, "It's showtime! Everyone backstage. I'm going to open the doors and let the audience in." Pretty soon the audience has been seated, the lights go on, and the curtain goes up.

Josh gives me a high five, and the play starts.

Things go okay until it's time for my important scene. I realize I have a problem, and it's a big one. My furry tail is *stuck*! It's stuck on one of the roots of the big tree in the center of the forest. And the roots are really just the metal legs of the round table from the teachers' lounge wrapped in brown paper and duct tape, so it's stuck good. I need help, or I won't be able to make my offering to the King and Queen of the Forest and say my brand-new lines. I look around for help. Makayla is closest.

"Psst, Makayla! Help me disconnect my tail. It's caught on this root!" I say.

"Lola, I'm about to present my fairy

flowers!" Makayla says. "Leave me alone!" Then she flits over to the king's and queen's thrones, flaps her sparkly wings, and offers her basket of flowers with a bow.

"Queen Arden, I give you these flowers to nurture and grow," Makayla says. "And I pledge the loyalty of fairies from high and low."

I'm starting to sweat in my fur. I try to get my tail out from under the tree, which starts to tilt. It takes all my soccer muscles to make sure it doesn't fall over.

The bluebirds flap over to Josh and Alyssa, the king and queen.

"A gift for you, our beautiful queen! A song of happiness to fill the forest green."

The bluebirds start to sing, and sweat

is dripping from my forehead. I have only until the end of the song to unhook my tail. The song ends. Improvise, I think.

"Greetings, Queen Arden, from your bushy-tailed friend!" I say from near the back of the stage. No one can see me, but luckily, I have a loud voice. I keep tugging as I talk.

"I come with a basket of nuts to lend." I don't know what to do, but I want Queen Arden to get her gift, so I come up with an idea. I pick up an acorn and toss it over the bluebirds' heads toward the thrones. I hear it hit the floor, so maybe I missed the horn of plenty holding the gifts. I try again.

"OUCH!" I hear Alyssa say in a not-very-queenly voice. "You hit me in the head!" Now everyone is moving away from me, and suddenly the audience can see me. I'm sweating and pulling, and my tail is *not* coming unstuck. I need to think fast.

"Queen Arden, I'm sorry I hurt thee, but my tail is stuck on the root of this tree!"

I toss the last two acorns, and this time, Josh is prepared. He jumps up and catches them.

"A present from us squirrels...," I start to say, and then—*riiiiiip!*—I fall down on all fours. "Ouch! My knee!"

There is a gasp in the audience. Then Olivia points to the place where my tail is supposed to be.

"There's a hole in her pants!" she says. I feel the air on my skin and know she's right. *What* am I going to do?

Then I hear it. A loud, dramatic voice. "My squirrel is hurt!" It's my *bubbe*. I think of her crazy peacock shawl.

"Grandmother Peacock!" I say. "Come with your shawl and save the day!"

"I'm coming, my squirrel," says Bubbe as she makes her way to the front of the gym. "Out of my way!"

All of a sudden, I hear Josh.

"Um, Grandmother Peacock!" he says. "Welcome to our forest. Do you have a gift?"

Grandma Levine looks at Josh and looks at me and says, "Yes, young king, I do," and then she *throws* her peacock shawl

over everyone's heads toward me. I catch it, of course, because I am a goalie after all! I know exactly what to do. I wrap the shawl around my waist and turn to the audience.

"Thank you, Grandmother Peacock, your gift is sweet. Now"—I think fast—"you may go back to your seat." Bubbe bows and then walks back to my family, whom I see smiling and grinning.

Josh walks forward and takes my hand and says, "Thank you, Squirrel. Our forest gifts are a wonderful sight. They will get us through the long winter nights."

Josh and I take a big bow and walk offstage. We are laughing so hard, we almost don't hear the applause.

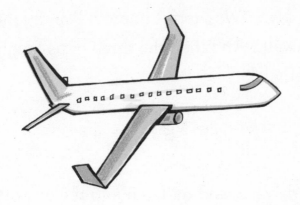

Chapter Eight
Bye-Bye, Bubbe

Principal Blot, Grandma Levine, and the rest of my family find us backstage.

"Lola! Zola! Granola!" Ben says. "That was awesome!"

Ms. Tinkle walks up to Josh and me

and says, "Wonderful improv! I've taught you well." And then the three of us laugh together.

We drive Grandma Levine to the airport a few days later, and we are all sad to see her go.

"Come back soon, Ruth," Mom says.

"Love you, Mom," Dad says.

"Bubbe," Ben says, "what's a kitty's favorite color?"

"I don't know," Grandma says.

"Purr-ple!" Ben says, and kisses Grandma good-bye.

I'm a little sad, so I just give Grandma Levine a big hug and tell her how much I

love her and how glad I am that she helped me out.

"Of course," Grandma Levine says. "Just remember, Lola, that not only are you dramatic, you are from a long line of DRAMA QUEENS!" And with a wave, she's off.

"I've got an idea," Dad says. "Let's go to the Ice Cream Palace!" Ben and I cheer.

"But no bubble-gum blowing contests, Benito!" says Mom.

"I promise," he says.

Dear *Diario*,

It's been a pretty crazy couple of months. First I learned about drama, then I got stage fright, then I got stage brave, and then I learned to improvise by throwing acorns across the stage in front of a couple hundred people. Most importantly, I learned that I have the best *bubbe* in the whole wide world—one who will fly across the sky just to give me a hug when I'm feeling bad.

Finally, my little brother, Ben, didn't bug me even once this week. He's in a much better mood since he convinced Mom and Dad to take him to the hairdresser, where he cut off *all* his hair. He wanted to match Mira. Mom says we are a very *dramatic* family and that's okay. We also have *extremely* much fun together.

If being dramatic means our inside voices sound like some people's outside voices, then that's okay with me.

Of course, that's just my opinion, and I have *lots* of opinions.

Shalom,
Lola Levine, Soccer
(and Drama) Queen

31901059525651